FOG PLANET

by Sally Odgers

illustrated by Georgina Thomas

This 2009 edition published in the United Kingdom by
Scholastic Ltd
Villiers House
Clarendon Avenue
Leamington Spa
Warwickshire
CV32 5PR

First published in 2007
by Macmillan Education Australia Pty Ltd.

Text by Sally Odgers
Illustrations by Georgina Thomas
Cover Design Allison Parry
Design by Matt Lin/Goblin Design
Managing Editor Nicola Robinson

Out of this World: Fog Planet
ISBN 978 1407 10113 2

Printed by Tien Wah Press, Singapore

1 2 3 4 5 6 7 8 9 9 0 1 2 3 4 5 6 7 8

Contents

Characters

The Arkies

Singer

Gentle Singer can sense the mind of any living being, and communicate by thought alone. She understands many languages.

Lyam

Science whiz Lyam can tell the Arkies everything they need to know about alien plant and animal life – and then some.

Merlinna

Merlinna is always ready for a battle. She's an expert with weapons – including her naturally piercing screech.

Pace

Pace is a practical guy with a very practical skill – he can communicate with electronic equipment. He and Singer are special friends.

EarthNet

Tench and Farla are EarthNet agents who trail the *Ark3*. They want to capture the Arkies and return them to Earth.

chapter 1

Cloud Cover

A*rk3* had been orbiting the cloud-covered planet for hours, and we were fed up.

"Aren't we ever going to land?" Merlinna can yell louder and glare harder than anyone I know. Now she glared at me. "Pace, make ArkMa do something."

I touched the console where *Ark3*'s electronic brain is. We call her ArkMa, because she's like a mother. We kind of love her, but she tells us stuff "for our own good". Especially me.

"ArkMa?" I said.

"Hello, Pace."

"ArkMa, we gotta get down on that planet sometime."

"I advise against it, Pace. Cloud cover is one hundred per cent," said ArkMa.

"It's been like that for hours. C'mon, Ma, take us down."

"If you insist!" ArkMa sounded huffy.

The deck dropped out from under my ship-boots and I fell against the console.

"Oops, sorry!" said ArkMa. She didn't sound at all sorry.

We all grabbed for the edge of the viewscreen as we spun out of orbit. ArkMa was right. Outside there was nothing but a thick quilt of clouds.

"Singer?" said Lyam. "You get anything yet?"

Singer is our psychic and linguist. If it breathes and thinks, Singer can talk to it. If it thinks and doesn't breathe, I can talk to it. Singer and I make quite a team.

Singer closed her eyes. "There's something alive out there," she said. "I can't get a clear reading."

That didn't sound good.

I was about to ask ArkMa to take us up again when we hit the ground – hard. I tripped and bit my tongue but there was no point complaining. ArkMa had advised against landing in thick cloud.

My eyes watered. I saw Singer's fingers turn white as she gripped the viewscreen. "It might be from EarthNet." Her voice was worried.

It had better not be, I thought. The people from EarthNet are always getting in our way. They pretend they want to send us back to Earth for our own good. What they really want is to close down the Arkie Exploration programme and use the money to build more boring space stations.

Merlinna lifted her chin. "Whether it's them or not, I'm going to explore."

Lyam tapped in the hatch code and ArkMa checked her sensors and printed out her initial report.

Merlinna opened the hatch. "Way to go, ArkMa. We nearly hit a cliff on the way down."

"Perfecto," I said quickly. I didn't want ArkMa to get any huffier. "That means *Ark3* won't be visible from at least one side." I patted the console. "ArkMa is looking after us."

"Looking after you, you mean." Merlinna sniffed the air. "Smells kind of damp ... bring the MatCon, Pace."

The MatterConverter is the key invention that makes the Arkie programme possible. Old-time space flights had to carry everything with them. But with our MatCon we are able to make things quickly from the materials on hand and it is easy to make contact with ArkMa. Most people have to dial in a code but I just point, tell the MatCon what I want and press. What people don't understand is that machinery is alive. It's just a different kind of life from ours. I picked up our MatCon and felt it purr with glee. It was ready for anything.

"Let's go, little bro!" I said to it quietly.

Leaving ArkMa to mind the ship, we Arkies stepped on to the surface of the planet. Singer and Lyam led the way. They couldn't see any better than Merlinna and me but they're better at sensing danger from carbon-based life forms.

(That means plants, animals, people and things, in case you didn't know.)

"This fog's a real blinder," I said. The cloud was one hundred per cent, right down to the ground.

"Good," said Merlinna. "If we can't see, neither can anything else. Lyam? Is this place S-R?"

Lyam sneezed. "I don't know, but there's some vegetation."

That was good news. To be S-R, Settlement-Ready, planets need to have oxygen, vegetation, water and metal. They should not have didgies or intelligent inhabitants.

I bumped into Lyam as he stopped to touch some plants. I caught a whiff of something bitter and Lyam sneezed again.

"Thad's nod good," he muttered. "I need a hagger-cheef." He held up a huge leaf. I focused quickly and gave it a burst with the MatCon. The leaf wove itself into a piece of cloth and Lyam blew his nose. "Nod deadly," he said, snuffling, "but nod good."

"Shh," hissed Singer.

Lyam blew his nose again and I used the MatCon to turn the handkerchief back into a

leaf. We're supposed to reverse conversions when we've finished with them. It's the right thing to do – and it helps confuse EarthNet agents. I hoped they hadn't made it to this corner of the galaxy.

We set off away from the foot of the cliff, sliding and scuffling over the rocks. After I fell over for the third time, I called a halt. "We gotta adjust these boots," I said. Soft-soled ship-boots just didn't cut it on this kind of surface.

A burst of the MatCon fixed that. We still couldn't see more than two steps in front of us, so I turned the MatCon to low beam. Later, I wished I hadn't done that.

chapter 2

Something in the Fog

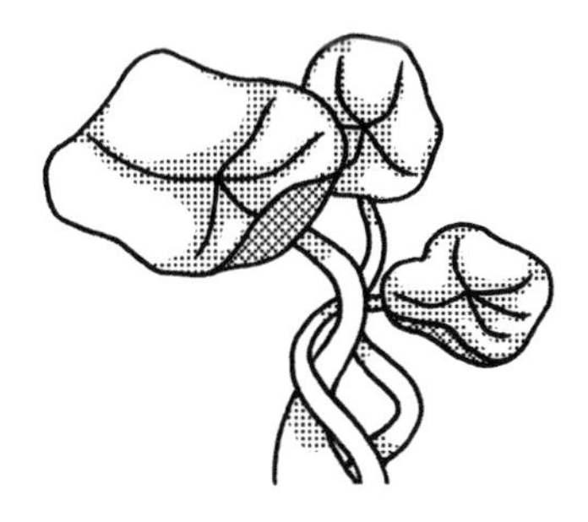

Even with the MatCon beam, we had to go slowly. Lyam collected samples of different plants and stowed them in his pouch. I experimented, turning rocks into tools.

"There's metal here," I said, showing Merlinna the knife I had made. Not even I can get a MatCon to make metal objects if there's no metal in the rock.

Merlinna took the knife. "It looks more like a pendant than a knife. Better give it to your girlfriend."

So it wasn't a very big knife. So what? And Singer isn't my girlfriend – not exactly. I took it from Merlinna and stuck it in my pouch. I'd have to find a bigger hunk of metal-bearing rock. I kept working as we moved, remembering, mostly, to unconvert the things that didn't work. The MatCon was having a great time. I could feel it fizzing with glee.

I walked into Lyam – again.

"You gotta stop stopping so suddenly, dude," I said.

Lyam reached back and stuck his hand over my mouth. It tasted as bad as the plants on this planet smelled.

"Shhh!" Lyam stopped Singer and Merlinna as well. "Did you hear that?"

"What?" Now we'd stopped walking, I could hear myself breathing.

"There's something in the fog."

I held my breath. Nothing. "Nah," I said.

"Singer?" said Lyam. "Any didgies here?"

A didgie is what we call the indigenous inhabitants of a planet. Singer and Lyam and Merlinna and I are didgies of Earth.

"I don't know." Singer sounded worried. "There's something..."

We waited a few more heartbeats, listening in every direction. Finally, Lyam relaxed. "Must be imagining things."

SSSSSSSSSSS SS
Ark3
Ark3

"Maybe Fog Planet didgies are made of fog," I said.

"I don't like this place," said Singer. "Fog Planet's a good name for it."

As she spoke, the fog began to lift.

As the surroundings came into focus, it was like seeing a holoviz warming up to show a film. The fog didn't go completely, but we couldn't see any didgies.

"It's all grey," said Singer.

She was right. The rocks were a dull grey, and so were the plants that had made Lyam sneeze. They were skinny and looked as if they were made of wire. The leaves were weird flat things that sat like saucers in a cradle of twisted stems.

"Why are they like that?" I asked.

"They're maximizing their exposure to light and moisture," said Lyam. He sounded like a textfile back in Arkie Academy. In case you don't know, that's where everyone chosen for the Arkie Exploration Programme goes for training.

It wasn't dark but it wasn't light either. Think of the stormiest day you can remember, in the

late afternoon, in the middle of winter, and you'll get an idea of how well we could see.

"Those leaves must fill with water when it rains," I said.

"If it ever does..." said Lyam.

Talking about rain made me thirsty. I used the MatCon to turn one of the leaves into a bowl and then converted some cloud into free water. It didn't taste good.

We walked on, keeping watch on all sides. Lyam was still convinced something was stalking us, but the fog-didgies – if that's what they were – stayed out of sight.

So did everything else. As far as we could see, everything was the same colour on Fog Planet. Grey rocks. Grey soil. Grey plants. The cliff where we had left *Ark3* was the only landmark, and that was out of sight now.

Finally, Lyam stopped. "These plants I've been sampling are identical," he said. "There's no variation in species, and you know what that means."

We did, but Lyam told us anyway. "The soil is so specialised it will probably grow only these

plants. Not many Earth-type food-plants can grow in such low light."

"Could be just a dull day," suggested Merlinna.

"This is as bright as it gets," said Lyam. "You can tell by the plants. No direct sunlight. No free rainfall. No wind."

I hoped Merlinna wouldn't ask how he knew there was no wind. Once Lyam is in geek-lecture mode it's hard to get him out.

"Let's tag this planet as non S-R, and leave," I said. "Who'd want to settle here?"

"OK by me," said Lyam. "Singer? Merlinna?"

The girls nodded. We Arkies always make decisions as a team. No one can ever blame anyone else if a decision goes bad.

We were about to turn back when the fog swooped over us again, thicker than ever. I couldn't see my hand in front of my face. I shone the MatCon beam at the ground, but all I could see was white stat-dazzle.

We couldn't walk in that, so we made camp.

I used the MatCon to convert some plants into enough canvas to make tents and then fizzed some more with air so we wouldn't have to sit on the ground. Next, I converted some leaves into food. Lyam was right – they weren't good to eat and it took a lot of leaves to get enough even half-eatable carbs. It tasted like MatCon food always does – bad.

We talked for a while, but the silences stretched until no one was answering. I was about to go to sleep when I realised one of us should stay on guard … just in case there really were hostile didgies in the fog.

chapter 3

Chain Time

When the fog lifted a bit, I woke the others. "Time to go," I said.

"We still can't see," objected Merlinna. She's our tracker, but even trackers like to see the ground.

"We'll use the MatCon. I'll get a fix on ArkMa right now." Since ArkMa and the MatCon are both electronic, I can use one to tune into the other.

I picked up the MatCon and waited for its little silent chuckle as it got ready for work. Nothing happened. "That's weird," I said. I shook the MatCon a bit and aimed it at the tent. The tent went on looking like a tent.

"Quit messing about, Pace," said Merlinna. "Unconvert those plants."

I held the MatCon up to my ear but it might as well have been a hunk of rock. "It's not working," I said. "I'd almost say the power pack had drained..."

"Impossible!" said Merlinna with a snort. "It's self-charging."

She was right, but Lyam went into geek-mode again. "Sure, it's self-charging, Merlinna, but what charges it?"

"Solar energy or wind power," I answered. (I knew that much.) Then I said "Oh" because I understood.

"You know what that means," said Lyam.

"Yes," Merlinna and I chorused, but Lyam told us anyway.

"It can't charge on this foggy planet. There's no sunlight and no wind."

This was really bad. If only I hadn't used the MatCon so much! If only I hadn't bothered with tents and mattresses and food! I glanced at the tents again. I'd have to leave them as they were. And that wasn't even the worst of it.

"Singer?" I said. "You got an update on those fog-didgies?"

Singer shook her head. "There's something thinking somewhere but it could be a hundred metres away – or in orbit."

The didgies had a ship? I extended my mind as far as I could but, as far as I could tell, there wasn't a live bit of machinery anywhere nearby. I couldn't even sense ArkMa without a boost from the MatCon. The fog was confusing me as badly as it did Singer.

"You're lost," said Merlinna.

She was right. There was no point waiting for someone to find us. We had to make our own way back but, with no MatCon and no sun or stars to steer by, that wasn't going to be easy, even with Merlinna's tracking skills. And when we did get back – what?

Merlinna cast around the tents. "This way," she said. "See? Pace has dropped one of his lumps of horrible leafbread and I just trod on a bit of his messed-up metal."

"Can you get us back?" asked Lyam.

"Sure," said Merlinna. "You picked leaves along the way, so we can follow the broken stems."

"And can we get into *Ark3* without the MatCon?" persisted Lyam.

"I expect Pace can get ArkMa to let us in," said Singer.

I sure hoped so.

We had to move in a tight bunch so as not to get separated and that meant falling over one another a lot.

The third time it happened, I laughed. No one asked what was funny but I told them anyway. "Arkies are supposed to leave no trace of where we've been but if we hadn't left these traces, Merlinna couldn't have backtracked us."

No one commented, so I added, "And we're explorers – pathfinders of the galaxy! We've come countless light years – and we're lost just half a day's walk from our ship." I laughed again.

That got more silence. I was about to say something more when Singer suddenly grabbed my arm. "Sssh!"

We all froze, listening.

Then we all heard it: a faint echo of sound.

Huhuhuhu.

"Who's there?" demanded Merlinna.

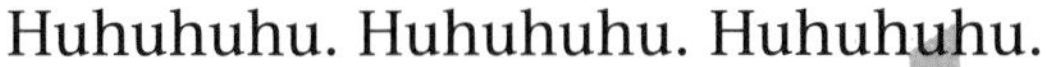

There was no answer, unless you counted a repeat of the same sound.

Huhuhuhu. Huhuhuhu.

"Is there someone there?" asked Merlinna.

Huhuhuhu. Huhuhuhu. Huhuhuhu.

"We'll take that as a yes, then," I said. I get smart-mouthed when I'm nervous.

"Show yourself!" Merlinna's voice never wobbled. I heard the snicking sound as she unlocked the tangle-line attached to her wrist. While we were at Arkie Academy I made the mistake of saying once that the tangle-line didn't look like much of a weapon. Merlinna let me have it around the legs.

Trust me. It's not an experience I want to repeat.

Huhuhuhu. Huhuhuhu. Huhuhuhu.

It sounded like the chuckle of a stream, but there was no stream here.

Then I thought I saw something falling through the mist. I was still trying to make it out when something clattered on stone fifty metres away.

"It's a fog-didgie," I said to Singer.

I heard Singer breathe in deeply and knew she was reaching out to whatever was making the sound. She was still gripping my arm, and I felt her squeezing tighter. Then my ears buzzed and I felt her voice inside my head.

Pace – chain time.

If we link our hands to make a chain Singer can talk in our heads. But she knows I hate chaining, so she does that only in real emergencies.

I felt her slide her hand down to mine. In an emergency, I don't ask questions, so I sneaked my other hand forward to brush my fingers against Lyam's. I braced myself. My ears itched. So did my eyeballs. My teeth felt strange.

Lyam – chain time, said Singer. Her voice passed through my body like static electricity. I felt Lyam twitch. He must have reached forward to take Merlinna's hand, because in another second Singer gave us all the news.

EarthNet agent landed at twelve o'clock high. Run. Now!

Ark3
Ark3
Ark3

chapter 4

Captured

EarthNet agents don't kill the Arkies they catch. They just send them on a one-way trip back to Earth to get "re-educated" in a nice place with bars on the windows. They hope if they can get rid of enough of us they can get the government to stop the Arkie Programme and let them have the money it costs for their own programme.

That's why we ran. We might have got away, if I hadn't fallen over a rock. It knocked the wind out of me and I banged my chin – hard. Arkie training means we're tough and strong but that hurt.

"Ooof!" That's all I said, but the EarthNet agent heard me. The light of a MatCon splashed over my head and then I felt a high-heeled ship-boot land in the middle of my back, pinning me down.

I could hear the others still running but the agent called them back.

"Your friend has fallen over, kids."

I groaned at the rock under my chin. I knew that voice. It was Farla Fettleman. She looked like anyone's grown-up sister and she had cute blond curls. Of all the EarthNet agents I knew, she and her partner, Tench, were the worst.

"Come on, kids, do come back!" She sounded as if she was smiling. "I need you to hold the light so I can help this boy up. I'd hate to tread on him by mistake."

As she spoke, she put more weight on the foot she had on my back.

"Ouch!" I said loudly, to tell the others she was lying. "She's treading on me already!"

"Oops! Is that better?" Farla trod a bit harder. I snaked my hand around to grab her ankle but she was wearing heel-spurs, and all I got were some sore fingers.

"Oh dear, he's hurt himself on my boot," said Farla. "But it doesn't have to be this way. Sit up, Pace ... it is Pace, isn't it?"

HA HA HA HA!

I gritted my teeth. She knew perfectly well it was me.

She leaned over and pulled my collar so my chin came off the ground. "I don't want to hurt you, Pace," she went on.

"You don't call choking me on my own collar hurting me?" I said. (Told you I get smart-mouthed when I'm nervous.)

"All I want is to talk some sense into you. You kids shouldn't be here. Look, Pace, I know being an Arkie seems really adventurous and clever to you now, but when you're older you'll understand. We just can't have you roaming around interfering with other planets. It isn't right."

"We don't interfere," I said. "If there are didgies on a planet, we leave."

"I'm sure that's what you think happens," said Farla, "but your Ark Masters don't leave it at that. No, no. As soon as you've left, they send in their terra-formers and within a few days the didgies are gone like that." She clicked her fingers. "It isn't right, the way they use you children to do their dirty work."

I snorted. I'd heard it all before and it was so not true.

"Our ship's overhead. We'll signal it and take you home," said Farla.

Farla must have come down in a yo-chute. Much easier than landing on a foggy planet.

"*Ark3* is our home," I said.

"We'll take you to a nice place where you can learn some really useful work."

"You've gotta be joking, right?" I muttered.

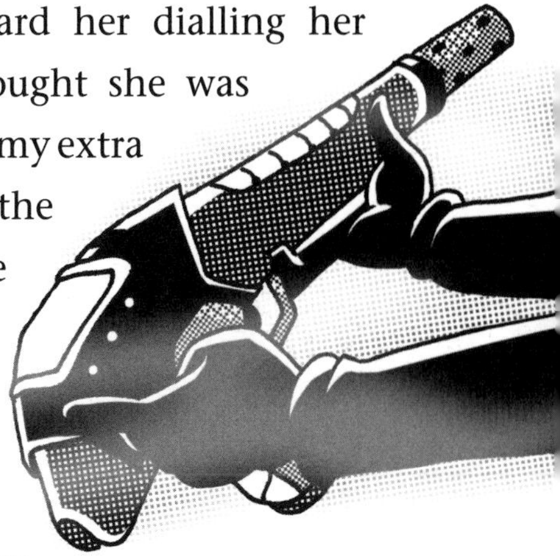

Farla laughed. I heard her dialling her MatCon. At first I thought she was keying the yo-chute for my extra weight, then I counted the clicks and realised she was making rope. She must plan to tie me up and then catch the others, so she could 'chute us all at once. She couldn't do it alone, so I figured her partner, Tench, had dropped as well. I hoped he hadn't staked out *Ark3*. ArkMa could keep him out – but he could keep us away from the ship.

Quickly, I made contact with Farla's MatCon. I longed to get my hands on it but it was way out of reach. Instead, I pictured the rope as the MatCon wove it from the nearest bush. I persuaded it to be loosely woven and stretchy. *Hang looooose, little bro,* I told it.

The MatCon seemed uncertain. I hoped it would follow my orders and not Farla's.

Farla was still chatting away, pretending to help me up. What she was really doing was putting her knee in the middle of my back while she tied my hands behind me.

That's when I saw another MatCon beam in the fog. Tench! He must have landed a few hundred metres away.

"Look out!" I yelled at the others but Singer and Lyam yelped as Tench grabbed them from behind.

You've gotta be thinking we were weak to let ourselves be caught like that. All I can say is, hey, you've never met Farla and Tench. Farla has the pointiest ship-boots ever made, and Tench is the biggest Earth didgie I've ever seen. He can crack nuts with his eyelids.

I hoped he wouldn't crack any Arkies with his bare hands.

Farla looped rope round my knees and tied it. She left me trussed up while she headed for Tench.

"Have you got the others?" She'd dropped the sweet voice now.

"Sure," said Tench. "One in each hand."

Farla clicked her tongue angrily. "That means there's still one loose. Tie those up, then we'll hunt the fourth."

I twisted my wrists around and felt the rope stretching and tearing. *Great work, little bro,* I thought towards Farla's MatCon. As I untied my legs, I watched its beam bobbing towards Tench and the others.

That's when Merlinna let out a yell that would have deafened a Spiral Nine Ear Bug and hit Tench around the legs with her tangle-line.

chapter 5

Chain Again

Tench yelled nearly as loudly as Merlinna and I felt the ground shake as he fell. His MatCon sailed through the fog and bounced.

"Singer? You OK?" I called.

I scuttled towards the fallen MatCon. I dived to grab it and cracked my head against what felt like a very lumpy rock.

The rock bellowed with pain, so I guess it was really Tench's head. I hoped it hurt him more than it hurt me but I wasn't betting on it.

"Singer? You OK?" I yelled again. "Where are you?"

I could hear lots of people rolling about in the fog – but who was who?

ZZZZZTT!

Zzzzzzzttt! That was Merlinna scoring another hit with the tangle-line and, from the way her victim yelled, I knew it was Farla.

I felt someone's fingers close round my ankle but I didn't kick because I knew right away it was Singer.

Pace – chain time.

My ears and eyeballs itched. I scrabbled round as quietly as possible until I could grab Singer's hand. Crouching low, we sidled towards Tench's MatCon, which was still jolting around. I was sure Merlinna was there, probably pulling her tangle-line free from Farla. That's the only downside of the tangle weapons – you have to pull them back before you can use them again.

I grabbed her shoulder and felt Singer make contact. *Merlinna – chain time.*

Zzzzzzzttt! Merlinna shot the tangle-line out again. This time the person who yelled wasn't an EarthNet agent.

Great, I thought. Now we know where Lyam is. Merlinna must have reeled him in, because we heard his boots stumbling over the rocky ground.

Lyam – chain time.

For once I welcomed the buzz-itch of Singer's message link. It meant Merlinna had made contact with Lyam. Now we were all linked together.

Let's go, said Singer, so we moved away as quickly and quietly as we could.

We didn't go far. We weren't sure which direction to take and we didn't want to lead the agents to *Ark3*. With luck they'd decide we'd left and then leave themselves.

We crouched low against a big rock (which

I found by bumping into it) and watched Tench and Farla looking for us. We saw the gleam of their MatCon beams in the fog. We heard them arguing, too. They'd shifted to another language, so I didn't know what they were saying. Singer did, though.

They're going to outwait us, she told us through the chain. *They have MatCons for food and water and they think we must have lost ours.*

I rubbed my itching ears. "We might as well have. A drained MatCon's no good," I whispered.

"Not to them, either," said Singer.

I don't know which of us had the idea first. Chaining is like that. Whoever it was, the idea was suddenly in my mind. If our MatCon drained without sunlight and wind, then the EarthNet agents' MatCons would eventually do the same.

"Do they know?" I whispered to Singer.

She listened to whatever the agents were saying. "No. They think they can outwait us."

"No way," I said.

A few hours later, I wasn't feeling so sure. It was cold sitting in the fog, and we couldn't even talk much. There were creepy huhuhuhu sounds. I wondered how the agents were making them – and why.

"They've had a new idea," said Singer. "They're going to tempt us out."

Soon after, the white glow of the MatCon beams turned red. The agents were using them on heat-mode.

"Good!" I whispered. "That uses a lot of power."

Then the smell hit me and I swallowed. Remember, I hadn't had anything but MatCon food since we left the ship. Farla had real food: dehydrated pizza! She was steam-hydrating it and I could smell the cheese and pepperoni bubbling. I felt myself starting to drool and my stomach rumbled.

That's so not fair! I thought.

Farla and Tench took their time eating that pizza and then they brewed up some vanilla coffee and wafted fresh-baked cake smell at us. I put my head in my arms.

"May as well get ourselves comfy," said Farla loudly. "I'll make us a couple of good chairs, and what about some of that chocolate cake?"

Chocolate!

We had real food on *Ark3* but it was weeks since I'd tasted chocolate cake.

"Farla's yo-chute will overload if she eats too much junk food," said Merlinna.

We waited – and waited. Every so often one of the agents would get up and cast around in a circle, shining the MatCon light among the rocks and plants. We knew they wouldn't see us if we held still.

"This is a waste of time," Tench said after a bit. "They've given us the slip."

"Not them." Farla raised her voice. "I can hear those hungry little tummies rumbling from here. They're too scared to move. Turn those MatCons back to red. It's cold and I want more pizza."

It was so quiet on Fog Planet that I heard the click of the dials as Tench twiddled them. The MatCon beams glowed red for a long while and then faded.

Yes! I thought ... and through the chain I heard Singer say it: *Yes!*

In a few seconds the EarthNet agents would be without food, water or light. They wouldn't be able to use their yo-chutes or even contact their ship.

The only problem was that we Arkies were in just the same situation!

chapter 6

Pace's Idea

While the agents were still trying to figure out what had happened, we moved cautiously away.

Unfortunately, Merlinna had lost the trail she'd been following when she'd rushed to attack Tench. We were experienced at navigating on strange planets but the thick fog made everything look the same.

We stumbled along but, for all we knew, we might be heading back towards our camp. By now I was seriously thirsty. I didn't like to think what might happen to us if we couldn't get back to *Ark3* soon. The Ark Masters would do their best to locate us but we were months out from old Earth. When they found us – if they found us – we might be nothing but bones.

So would the EarthNet agents, of course...

No! I thought. *We are going to get back to* Ark3. *All we have to do is keep searching until we find that cliff. We know it's within a few hours' walk.*

If our MatCon would work, that would be nothing. Even an old-fashioned compass would have guided us back to *Ark3*. I suppose you're wondering why we didn't carry one? Why would we? MatCons were much more versatile. Carrying a compass when you have a MatCon would be

like using a rock to drive in a nail when you have a multi-tool in your pouch. Why would you?

Now then, Pace, I thought. *One thing the MatCon hasn't replaced is your brain! Use it!*

I started putting things in logical order:

1. We were in the same position as Farla and Tench.

2. Lyam had figured out why our MatCon wasn't charging.

3. The agents didn't seem to know what was wrong with theirs.

Surely we could take advantage of that, somehow?

I was so busy thinking I stubbed my toe and tripped – again – dragging Singer down with me. I banged my fingers against a rock. "Ouch!" I said and blew on them.

Got it!

I felt a big grin forming on my face as I helped Singer up.

"What?" You can't keep secrets from Singer. She could tell I'd had an idea.

"We need to make artificial wind to charge the MatCon," I whispered, and blew on my fingers to demonstrate.

"Blow on it?" She sounded surprised. "That won't work, Pace."

"I know what will! Merlinna, can I borrow your tangle-line?"

"No," said Merlinna.

"Aw, come on. I need it."

Merlinna told me exactly why a clumsy person like me should never use a tangle-line.

"I need it," I said, and explained why.

"I'll do it," said Merlinna.

"No." I wasn't just being stubborn. I had a gut feeling that, if anyone could recharge a MatCon this way, it would be me.

Reluctantly, Merlinna handed me the tangle-line. I pulled out the tip and tied it around the

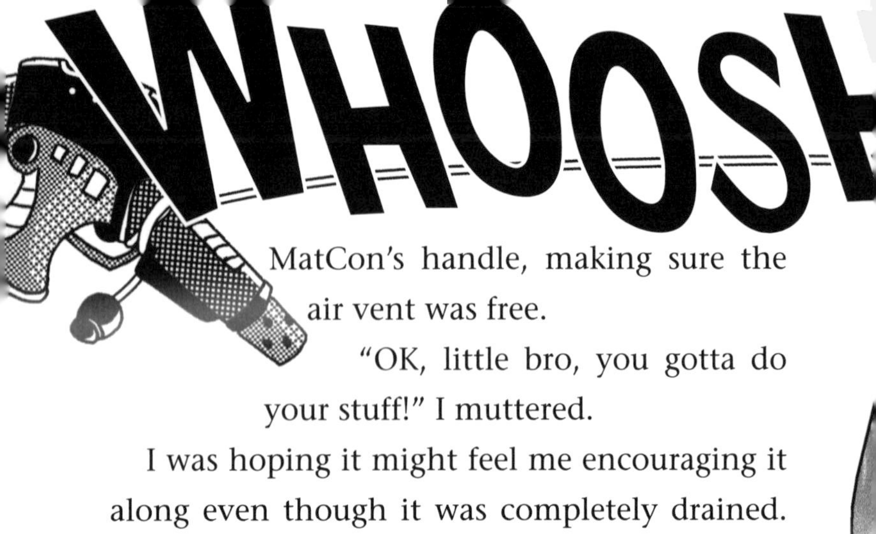

MatCon's handle, making sure the air vent was free.

"OK, little bro, you gotta do your stuff!" I muttered.

I was hoping it might feel me encouraging it along even though it was completely drained. Then, just in case the tangle-line felt left out, I encouraged it as well. "C'mon, line, show me what you've got!"

"Stand clear," I instructed the other Arkies.

Merlinna had already backed away and Lyam and Singer followed. I moved clear of the rock.

I tested the tangle-line with my fingers, then gripped it a metre from the end and whirled it around my head. The weight of the MatCon made it swing smoothly. I felt like an old-style cowboy spinning a rope.

Deciding to put some muscle in it, I let out more line, leaned on my heels and swung as hard as I could.

Art3
Art3

That's when my teeth began to vibrate. My ears prickled and my eyeballs itched. It felt as if Singer was chaining again but she was standing well back with the others in the fog.

Imagination, I thought, gritting my teeth, but the harder I swung, the worse it felt. Finally, I realised the MatCon was singing! The air blowing through the vent was making a very high whistling noise which was growing stronger all the time. It was whistling through the line and down into my bones.

"Yes!" I said. "It's charging! Perfecto!"

I wanted to rub my ears but I didn't dare to stop swinging. With luck, the MatCon would let me know when it was ready for work.

"What's that?" called Farla's voice. She was closer than I expected. "Pace, is that you?" She sounded as if her teeth were vibrating, too. I hoped so. I whirled the MatCon harder. If Farla didn't like the noise, I was prepared to love it.

Something pinged against my knee. For a second I thought the MatCon had somehow shocked me, then my cheek stung and I realised Farla was throwing stones. They were only pebbles, so I guess she didn't want to harm me – much.

I winced when a bigger pebble smacked into my shoulder. If she kept this up, I'd have to stop. If Tench joined in...

Then Tench did join in. I yelped with pain. This was serious.

chapter 7

Hullabaloo

Another high whine started up, from somewhere over to my left.

My teeth buzzed and I shivered. Had Farla started swinging her MatCon too?

Ouch!

Not unless she could swing and throw pebbles at the same time.

The whine from my left shifted up a notch and suddenly I knew what it was.

Merlinna has the kind of voice that can shatter crystal when she's mad!

Now she was screaming on the same note the MatCon was using, moving about to confuse Farla and Tench.

YAAAARAAAAR!

It seemed to be succeeding, because no more pebbles hit me after that. Judging by the rattle of heel-spurs on rock, the agents were trying to get a fix on Merlinna. The MatCon sang louder. Maybe it liked Merlinna's screaming. I didn't – and it was about to get a whole lot worse.

From somewhere behind the agents, another wail started, sliding up the scale. The hair on the back of my neck was prickling by now. Another wail joined in from the right, and then another, until the whole of Fog Planet seemed to be whooping and whining around us in a terrible hullabaloo.

I knew it had to be some weird kind of echo-effect, unless Merlinna had learned how to throw her voice. An echo has to come from somewhere and I was pretty sure this one could come from only one place: the cliff where we'd left *Ark3*.

We must be closer than I'd thought. Despite the horrible noise, I grinned. Things were going our way at last!

I wasn't the only one feeling better. The MatCon's song had settled and I could feel it thrumming with energy. MatCon was charged and ready to work.

RGHHHHHGHHHH
HH!
RGHHH
Ark3
GHHH
HHHHHHH!

Perfecto! I pulled the tangle-line back in, untied it and took the MatCon in my hand. *Just a little direction, bro!* I requested. *We gotta say hi to ArkMa.*

I couldn't hear her from this distance, not with all the screaming, but I felt the click as the MatCon made contact. The green guiding light appeared. Now all I had to do was locate the others and head for home.

I found Lyam by falling over him. He was crouched with his fingers in his ears.

Then Singer found me. I touched her hand and it felt as cold as custard. She was shaking.

"It's OK now," I said, close to her ear. "The MatCon's working, so now we've just gotta find Merlinna."

"I'm here." Merlinna's hand came over my shoulder and took the tangle-line.

"Perfecto," I said, pitching my voice below the hullabaloo. I grabbed Singer's arm. "Let's go, dudes."

I stepped out, leading the way. Bits of me were hurting or itching, but I was feeling kind of good about myself as we left the agents behind.

That is, until something struck me.

If Merlinna was here with us, who was making all the noise?

✪ ✪ ✪

"If it wasn't you, who was it?" I asked, as ArkMa let us into the ship. She was annoyed with us for being out of contact but that would have to wait.

Merlinna looked tired. I guess none of us was at our best after our adventures on Fog Planet. It hadn't exactly been fun.

"It was me at first," she said. "I wanted to stop Farla throwing things at you." Before I could thank her, she added, "I was afraid she'd hit the MatCon."

"What good thinking," I mumbled.

"I thought Singer had joined in," said Lyam.

Singer shook her head. "No, it wasn't me. It was the fog didgies."

"What?" I stared at her.

She shrugged. "Remember that funny huhuhu sound? And the other things Lyam heard?"

"That was Farla and Tench," I said.

"No it wasn't. We heard Farla land, remember?"

I couldn't think of an answer to that. But … fog didgies? "We never saw any fog didgies," I protested.

"No, but we all heard them." Singer grinned suddenly. "No wonder I couldn't get a fix on them. They're kind of quiet but they seem to join in when they hear noises. That huhuhu – I think they were copying Pace's laugh."

"They sure scared me," said Lyam.

"And the agents," said Merlinna. "You think they'll get back to their ship?"

"Who cares?" I said.

Singer and Lyam looked at me and I held up my hands in surrender. "OK, OK. We can't leave them out there. It wouldn't be fair … to the fog didgies."

I set to work to dry out the MatCon so it would work properly. It would take an hour or so, I thought, or maybe a bit longer. I wanted Farla and Tench to have a nice lot of time to wonder if they'd ever get home... After that, ArkMa would hover us over their heads and we could tell them – from a safe distance – how to recharge their MatCons so they could get their yo-chutes working.

Of course, they didn't have a tangle-line, so they'd have to tear bits off their smart ship-suits to make a long enough rope.

I kind of liked that idea.

FOG PLANET
Official Arkie report.

Fog Planet Cosmopedia

Arkie Academy Where the Arkies learned their special skills.

Arkies Teenagers with special training who act as pathfinders, seeking new Settlement-Ready planets.

Ark3 The space craft in which the Arkies travel.

ArkMa The sentient computer that flies *Ark3*. A shipbrain.

Ark Masters The heads of the Arkie programme.

Chaining Singer uses chaining (mindtalking through linked hands) in an emergency.

Didgies Indigenous inhabitants of a planet.

Docking beacon A beacon to which a shipbrain like ArkMa can lock.

EarthNet An organisation that wants the Arkies to go home.

Hatch code The typed-in code that tells ArkMa to release the hatch.

Fog Planet Cosmopedia

MatCon Matter converters, used to convert matter into useful objects – including food. Can only work if the raw materials are present.

Ship-boots Footwear worn by Arkies and EarthNet Agents.

Shipbrain The electronic mind of an Arkie ship.

Ship-suit One-piece garment used by spacers.

S-R (Settlement-Ready) Planets that have oxygen, free water, vegetation, metal and no intelligent didgies.

Tangle-line Merlinna's weapon of choice. A flicked line that entangles legs or arms and stings but does not injure.

Viewscreen Viewing hatch aboard the *Ark3*.

Yo-chute An electronic line EarthNet agents use to travel up and down from their orbiting ships.